Jayne D

ONE MIND TWO HEARTS

AUSTIN MACAULEY PUBLISHERS™

LONDON • CAMBRIDGE • NEW YORK • SHARJAH

A CIP catalogue record for this title is available from the British Library.

ISBN 9781398492165 (Paperback)
ISBN 9781398492172 (ePub e-book)

www.austinmacauley.com

First Published 2023
Austin Macauley Publishers Ltd®
1 Canada Square
Canary Wharf
London
E14 5AA

Jayne Drennan was born in 1971. She spent her earlier years in the small Yorkshire village of Wombwell. At the age of 13, her family moved to Blackpool, Lancashire, to run a small guesthouse. Tragedy struck in 1990 when her mother died from breast cancer. As part of Jayne's grieving process, she found solace in writing. In her late 20s, Jayne was diagnosed with a Hydrocephalus and degenerative hearing impairment, again she took comfort in writing. Then the pandemic struck globally. Through those furloughed days, Jayne decided to complete one of her early works and *One Mind Two Hearts* was accomplished.

To my husband, Mark, for his time and patience while I was putting the finishing touches to this book and helping me achieve my goal. I love you with all my heart. To my dad, Arnold, who listened to every poem I ever wrote. And to our lovely grandchildren, Jenson and Tulip, who loved listening to crazy nana's stories, I love you lots.

One Mind Two Hearts is a story of love and a belief that there is hope and happiness after failure and sadness, and to always hang on to your dreams. Happiness seemed a million miles away from Freya and Brett, they had never met, never loved, or had they? For both of them, the night-time was a saviour, a place they could be together. When they closed their eyes, their dreams became their happiness.

Freya woke to the sound of the alarm tone ringing in her ears, 'another day another dollar,' she often said of herself each morning. Yet this morning felt different. She sat up and proclaimed loudly as she had done on many previous occasions, "What a shambles I have made of my life, things have got to change." Every day had become Groundhog Day to her, nothing changed or ever will. She ate the same breakfast, saw the same people, went to bed by 9.30 almost every night but not the weekend that was perhaps 10.30 or sometimes later. How very uninteresting life had become, it could not be any more boring or mundane!

Now Nick had left her, she had sunk into a depression not realising it had taken over her life. The once bubbly happy-go-lucky Freya had evaporated and been replaced by a sad and depressed thirty-something divorcee who no longer wanted to do anything. If it wasn't for her work, she probably would have stayed in bed all day, and she would have if she didn't need the money.

Her salary barely kept her afloat, but it paid the bills, provided a small glimpse of stability, and ultimately maintained a roof over her head. After all, it was Nick who had almost put her in financial ruin.

Don't go there, Freya reminded herself, *it will mess with your head again.* A place she did not want to return to especially given the heartache and total humiliation of what Nick had done to her.

She was deeply hurt and the pain was extremely raw. "Oh, yes, Nick," she mumbled to herself, "the ex-husband who turned out to be nothing more than a lying, cheating flea-bag of a human being." How could she ever trust again? So, this was Freya's life now, the daytime her enemy and the night time her comfort.

She felt safe indoors away from everyone and as the daylight faded and night-time darkness began to fall, her dream was her saviour, she was able to drift off into another life where no one would ever hurt her again.

At the same time, Brett woke with the same recurring dream; one he had been having for so many years. Who was she? Why was she so unhappy? He could see her so vividly each night as he slept, she had become a vital part of his life, always reaching out to him with sadness in her eyes. He named her 'angel of the night' as he had only ever seen her in his dreams. Brett wanted to take her in his arms and make love to her forever and it felt like he had another life with a mysterious woman.

He wanted to make her happy, make her smile, but she was not real, just a vision in his dreams. A very beautiful image, a beautiful person and a life he wanted so very much. He desperately wanted to live his dream and he wanted it so badly. It was completely taking over his thoughts and life. He could think of nothing else. There was nothing here for him anymore, his marriage was hanging by a thread, and he felt so alone. Brett knew he was being totally foolish and sometimes perhaps felt he was going crazy, maybe he was a little mad and a fantasist. But it was all he was clinging to in the hope that it would bring him happiness. He had fallen in love with a dream, a vision of the future, and it would not go away. Nor did he want it to.

Brett visited his doctor once but found it too embarrassing to explain his situation so he just told the doctor he felt depressed. It wasn't a lie, it was the truth and he had felt this shadow of gloom hanging over him for years. Brett said nothing to the doctor about the dreams he was having, it was far too complex to explain, he just didn't know where to start and to be honest, it was almost humorous and possibly a wee bit disturbing. Yet, he so much wanted to tell someone and let it all out, someone to listen to him and tell him he wasn't worthless and that he was normal and these thoughts were not strange or uncommon. He just sat there remaining quiet saying nothing perhaps it was for the best.

What if he told the doctor how he felt and the dreams he constantly had, maybe he might have been referred to for psychological evaluation or even sectioned never to be released again into society. And so he just came away with three months of prescribed medication and a follow-up appointment. The doctor explained he was suffering from mild depression which Brett already suspected was the case. He never did go for the pills and never went back for the follow-up. He felt guilty and a total jerk for wasting the doctor's time.

He gave a wry smile as he left the surgery, was it depression, was he suffering from an obsession perhaps, even an overactive imagination or worse an anxiety attack of some sort? Still, Brett had to be grateful for the little happiness he had in life and the dream of 'Angel' was very much a part of that happiness. His mother Vivienne was still alive, although she was now in her mid-seventies and other than later life's ailments she was in reasonable health.

She had chosen to live out her days in a private assisted living rest home fortunately funded by his late father Jeremy from an investment pension he took in his 20s. She was a very well-respected wonderful woman. Brett loved her dearly and visited her regularly or whenever he was in the area, even on the odd occasion managing to visit her just to get out of the way of his wife 'Cheryl'.

He rarely visited his mum accompanied by Cheryl as she was overpowering and totally dominated the conversation which invariably was always about her or a subject which involved her. His mother had found this irritating and was pleased when Brett visited alone, although she never had the heart to tell her son, but thought he secretly knew.

Brett could easily talk openly with his mother as she was a very good listener; she never questioned, just listened and if he asked for advice, she gave it but only if Brett had asked. She remembered as if it was yesterday about the fallout, she and Brett had years ago when Brett's father was still alive, it was so painful for her to not see and talk to her only child for over a year. She vowed never to give opinions to her son again and she never did. But Vivienne believed she would be proven right and knew Brett was making a mistake in marrying Cheryl. She had openly discussed the situation with Jeremy but he firmly told her, "Vivienne darling, do not interfere in our son's life it will only cause heartbreak." Sadly, he was right. So she watched her son make a mistake and it tore her apart. Brett was about to marry the woman she knew would never make him happy. He was far too young to marry at twenty-two, he had his whole life in front of him; he needed to live more, travel and see the world.

Vivienne pleaded with Brett and begged him at that time not to marry so soon. "Date for a while, get to know one another better, anything but don't marry now, son, it's far too soon."

Her advice had fallen on deaf ears for he was blinded by love, beauty and sex appeal and the pressure from Cheryl to get married. Brett knew Cheryl could have any man she wanted, she was stunningly beautiful and he certainly wasn't going to lose her to anyone else. And so he agreed to marry her.

Now as her son sat beside her with sadness and sorrow in his eyes, she knew she was right fifteen years earlier and Brett knew it too. Vivienne held his hand tightly and whispered, "Son, it is never too late to change direction and follow your dreams, you are still young enough to start again. I am not going to live forever and my only wish is to see you happy. I love you, son, so very much, please follow your heart and I believe it will take you to the right place. You have been alone and lonely for too long, now it is time for you to make a change, think of yourself for once, Brett, put yourself first it is your time, now be brave my son and follow your dream. You know if I can help you in any way, you only have to ask, I will always be here for my son, always." Brett knew his mother was right and even back then in those earlier fallout days, she was right, but he was too much in love to admit it.

"Thanks, Mum," Brett whispered as he hugged her and held her tightly.

A small tear fell softly down her cheek. Maybe now he would appreciate her advice from those years ago. Let's just call it 'a mother's intuition'.

Brett never told anyone about his dreams; how could he explain it? And how would he explain to Cheryl, his wife of fifteen years, how he had fallen in love with a woman in his dreams? This was Brett's secret; it had to be; people would think he was mad, fantasising over a vision in his dreams, and they would be right; he was, but to Brett, it was real and it was his dream, and no one could ever take that from him. If Cheryl ever found out about his 'angel,' she may never visit him again, and his dreams would be lost forever. He could never risk that!

Freya drove to her work at the call centre along the usual route she took each morning: the same cars, the same traffic jams—how very boring. Her job was boring, she was boring, and she was sick of being stuck in this rut at the same office desk all day on the telephone trying to help endless people with their energy bills. It was such an uninspiring, boring job. It drove her mad to sit and stare at a despairing computer screen for eight hours a day. How could she change her life? She needed to get away; she was desperately unhappy with the choices she had made, and life was certainly not getting any easier. Too many mistakes had been made along the way. It was just deeply saddening to think about, and she didn't want to get any more upset at this time in her life.

Freya was used to laughing with her friends, 'big or bust,' gossiping about their next conquests, nice husbands, kids, holidays, and nice houses, and this had happened to nearly all of her friends; they had made the 'good' times, and she was happy for them. But not Freya. She had gone bust ('big time').

"Things will get better; they have to; they bloody well have to," she mumbled.

Freya knew she had to make different choices now and believe in herself, maybe taking a risk now and again to follow her dreams. She did not want to be alone anymore, even though she vowed never to be in another relationship and questioned if she could ever love again, as Nick had taken all the love she had. She swore she would never love again, but deep inside Freya knew and felt it in her heart that someone was there for her, someone to love and take care of her. It was a hope to cling onto, and it had helped her through the bad days.

Life was ticking by for Freya, it had been over five years since Nick left and she was still dwelling on self-pity. It had to stop. Clearly, choices had to be made, not by her friends, as she always seemed to do what they said. But she herself, now had to make those decisions, plan for the future and put those past dark days behind her once and for all. Too much time had been spent dwelling on Nick, far too long. Now at thirty-two, she had to wake up and plan her future.

Nick was a regrettable shit with a capital S, a massive ego and a huge pair of wandering eyes. She knew his reputation and despite all that, she went ahead and married him. What was the attraction? That bad boy image? Now the very thought of him made her angry that she could have been so stupid. All the warning signs were there, the big red lights flashing at her. Love took hold as well as security and a desire to belong to someone, someone to love and to be loved something she never had as a child. 'Pops' had passed away when she was just thirteen leaving her sad and vulnerable and she just did not want to be or feel alone anymore, just to feel loved.

She first met Nick seven years ago and couldn't believe her luck. He was charming, romantic, extremely handsome and just 'drop-dead gorgeous'.

Freya was the envy of most of her friends and she loved him very much. She always knew he was a flirt, after all, he had flirted with her at the cafe she worked at back in 2014. He had such a distinguishing appeal and for her the attraction was instant. She believed he had the same feelings for her. It wasn't a major concern that he was this self-confessed 'ladies' man'; after all, he was hers and they were going to be married, make babies and do what normal couples do. And so for over a year that is exactly what they did, enjoying every minute of the journey ahead.

It was deep in her memory when he proposed on the plane flying home after a fantastic weekend in Madrid. He had it all planned. Nick had the captain silence the whole plane while he got down on one knee and proposed, while the stewardess brought out champagne. She was totally smitten and spellbound, it was just so romantic.

Married life, at first, was really good, they had so many fun times and there was never any thought to question Nick where the money came from. After all, he had a great job working in a well-established firm of stockbrokers. He was a senior financial adviser and had several blue-chip clients and as such why would she be concerned as his high-end salary provided everything; money was never an issue. She had since packed in work at the cafe. Nick said that he could take care of her and that she did not need to work all those long hours. On Nick's advice, she took a part-time office job with a client of his just to provide her with some spending money. They had nice things and moved into a small two-bedroom detached cottage down by the canal; it was all she ever wanted. It was so different from her childhood.

Freya loved it. They had a whirlwind engagement; how could she refuse to marry Nick as he had given her the most magnificent two-carat diamond engagement ring, the likes of which she had only seen in some glossy magazine or on the finger of some famous celebrity? It was truly beautiful and no doubt very expensive.

Freya loved the bones of Nick and loved the attention he gave her; he made her feel so special. She had missed that so much in her childhood; it all just fell nicely into place. She accepted that he was a flirt and sometimes overly tactile with the ladies, but that was part of his charm and what attracted her in the first place. She could cope with that, but if she had only known, she would have run a mile. How was she to know it would all come crashing down on her and that her life would be turned upside down and inside out? She was totally lovestruck; just why had she not seen through the facade, the lies, and the deceit? It was so unfair; she did not deserve to be treated like this. Why do some people flourish through life and have a happy ever after? Why was that person not her? She felt like a failure (Freya sighed to herself). It was she alone who had made the choice to marry Nick; no one had held a gun to her head. We all make choices and decisions in life, good or bad. Freya remembered that this is what Dr. Alled, the psychologist she had visited following Nick's disappearance, once told her; unfortunately, at that time, it didn't sink in; nothing did, but now, thinking back to that time, Dr. Alled was right. Something always stuck with her at those meetings; the word "decision" always cropped up. We all have the right to decide; we all have choices, right or wrong; whatever you choose, you have to learn to live with them.

Brett took the train to work as usual, it was so much easier getting to the office by train and less stressful, it gave him time to think and relax for a while. Cheryl always took the car, public transport was beneath her, he had loved her so much when they had married and he never saw the selfishness in her, he was just so love-struck and happy to be with a young sexy woman who lit up the room. How happy they had been back then, and how lonely he had now become. He always gave in to Cheryl, he gave her whatever she wanted and tried so hard to please as he believed marriage was for life and yet something was missing in his life now 'ANGEL'. He wanted her so much, she was so beautiful, he wanted to kiss her, to run his fingers through her long black hair, but how could he, she was not real. Or was she? This had to stop as it was driving him nuts. Maybe he should visit a psychiatrist, he sometimes thought to himself, maybe he was crazy and needed help. He should have taken the doctor's advice and taken the pills, but then what if the dreams stopped? He couldn't imagine closing his eyes and never seeing her again. It was all he ever thought about. Now nothing else made him happy, but he had to face up to the fact that his life was with Cheryl, and he was going to spend the rest of his life in doom and gloom. She was after all the woman he had promised to spend his life with. It made him sad to think that he wanted to be with another woman rather than his wife.

He felt a betrayal, yet he compared them. Cheryl was blonde and beautiful, everyman's fantasy, but so petulant and very demanding 'I want, I want, I want' was a familiar refrain. She reminded him of the girl in the story *Just William,* 'I'll scream and scream and scream until I make myself sick' and yet always gave in, anything for a quiet life.

Cheryl had a nice sports car, expensive clothes, they had a nice home and a life of ease most people would envy. Brett had worked damn hard for it. He had built up a first-class reputation as a chartered quantity surveyor with many clients on his books some of whom were high-end property developers and as a consequence, this provided an excellent income. Cheryl was, however, a compulsive spender, so he had to work all the more harder to keep her in the luxuries she demanded. Nothing came cheap as she had become high maintenance. Cheryl didn't have any intention of working, no ambition for herself. She was now a kept woman and whatever it was she wanted she was having no questions asked and no thought of value!

She had it easy and had so for her entire life. It began in her early childhood. Cheryl was wrapped in cotton wool by her parents. She was spoiled and given the best of everything, her happiness was their utmost priority, and they sacrificed everything to give their child whatever she needed.

Clearly, this didn't help her later in life, she became even more demanding putting more pressure on Brett and he didn't realise he was sinking into a black hole and he seemed to be stuck there for a very long time. She never realised what she was doing to him, or even more so, she just didn't care. How different their worlds were and their upbringings; both were only children with loving parents, Cheryl was in a materialistic bubble and Brett was given love and attention, and was taught how to appreciate and understand values in life. Who is to judge which child is the best or who had the better childhood; it is all about preparing your child for the journey ahead and being a good, honest and caring person.

The only thing Brett knew was that Cheryl was an unappreciative and ungrateful person who had no respect for anyone let alone her own parents. He often thought they were a tiny bit scared of her and they did not realise they were creating a monster until things had gone too far, so they just carried on.

Brett's parents were totally opposite; they were lovely people and had great respect for them. He was devastated when his father Jeremy died suddenly aged sixty-two, his passing left him and his mother heartbroken. Brett was their only child and they doted on him. They had him later in life and called him their miracle baby. Brett believed he had a wonderful childhood, he could still hear his father's words, "Always be good, son, and help others, but most of all be kind."

Brett took that with him on his journey through life. He was totally opposite to Cheryl and on the other end of the spectrum, they really should never have met, and yet they say opposites attract. However, it appeared not true in their case, they were two totally different people. If there was to be a contest between them, he would win and get the trophy as his preparation in life had been mentored well and he had a lot to thank his parents for particularly the grounding that made him fully appreciate basic values. Material possessions were never his thing, it was all for Cheryl, she wanted the best of everything and she got it. That had now just become a normal life for Brett and he just slotted in somewhere like the last little piece of a jigsaw you wouldn't know it was missing, it just slotted in at the end without anyone noticing, that was him alright, the down-trodden man he had become, he just did not recognise himself anymore.

He wanted so much more for himself; he wanted the woman in his dreams; he wanted the vineyard he had always told his dad he was going to buy when he was a little boy; secretly, it had always been his father's dream, and Brett wanted to fulfil that for him. In his mid-to-late teens, they always visited the vines whenever they were on holidays, and Brett was completely fascinated by his dad's knowledge and love of well-nurtured grapes and, of course, a glass or two of excellently produced local wine. But most of all, he himself wanted to achieve that happiness and fulfilment.

He looked in the mirror and turned away. He just did not recognise himself anymore; his face was pale and pasty, and he had dark eyes. He was fading away into the abyss. How the hell did he end up like this? He had given it all in his marriage—blood, sweat, and tears—and was getting nothing back. Brett could remember the first time 'angel' came into his dreams; it must have been five years ago, but he could not pinpoint the exact time or how and why it happened. He was desperately unhappy and needed a break from everything. He had told Cheryl he had work commitments and needed to go away for a few days to tie up loose ends on a potential lucrative building project. He detested having to lie, but he needed some time away—time to think, time to sort out what was going through his head. Cheryl nodded in agreement, as it was work, something she avoided, and her tennis lessons would take priority. Brett was relieved she didn't try to tag along; the very thought of that depressed him.

They hadn't had sex for over a year and now slept in different rooms, and somehow Cheryl always seemed to have a headache. Nonetheless, he much preferred it that way.

He needed to love again, someone to hold, someone to care for, someone to share his dreams, and as he fell asleep that night in the small but cosy B&B bedroom, he saw her reaching out to him, pleading to not give up hope.

As he woke the next morning with a thick head, he saw the empty malt whisky bottle lying there and that depressed him even more, but he still remembered the dream, that beautiful face, and immediately his spirits lifted. He never envisaged this would be a recurring dream that would change his life forever.

Brett rang Cheryl that morning to say he would be staying another night at the hotel, contracts hadn't been completed and signed off due to a technicality and he had also been approached by a potential new client in the area, an opportunity he didn't want to miss. Of course, he, again, was lying but he just wanted another night to stay alone with his dreams. "Pick me up a surprise, Brett darling, you know how I love surprises." Cheryl to a 'T' as always only thoughts were about her. He wanted to say, enough, Cheryl, how many more surprises do you need? Little did she know the biggest surprise was about to unfold!

Brett just needed out, now he had to get away from this whole situation, change career, move on, and he often still thought of the vineyard he and his dad talked about, that small, picturesque vineyard somewhere in Greece somewhere quiet and peaceful. These were always part of his thoughts at times like this when he felt really low, but they were always pushed to the back of his mind after he married Cheryl.

But now, he started thinking more and more of starting afresh, suddenly it had become very appealing and when he closed his eyes, he could imagine he was there walking hand in hand with 'angel'.

"Stop," he yelled, "get a grip on yourself it was just a fantasy and an obsession within a dream." But why should he not like these thoughts, after all, it was his secret pleasure. Had he seen 'angel' in some passing place, some parallel universe or had he met her in a previous life? Did he believe in that (maybe), could she have been a lost love in another universe? Whatever it was he knew this woman and had a long desire to be with her. Brett had heard stories of reincarnation of how people could remember previous lives – was this happening to him? Did he have the powers to remember things, to see, to dream, to want to return to a previous life? This was crazy, he was crazy, he had to be. He had read many books on the afterlife, reincarnation, and patients who lay on shrink couches and go under regression through hypnosis to see if they have previously been here before. Surely, it all made sense to others, it was probably a mumbo jumbo but not for Brett; he was a believer (or a very deluded man). Sometimes Brett thought of internet searching some of the actual people from the books he had read. He wanted to hear their accounts first-hand, but that was a step too far.

If Cheryl had found out she would have ridiculed him for weeks and made him a laughing stock. Why the hell did he always put her feelings first? He was weak. It had always been the case, anything for a quiet life. He always said better to avoid an argument it's just not worth the hassle. He never won an argument anyway, he just bowed out and walked away, one of these days he would crack under the stress and Cheryl would always play the victim, she was good at that and not much else, but for her acting, she would win the best supporting actor award at the Oscars.

The more Brett thought of it, the more anger burnt in his belly. All he wanted to do right now was punch the wall and let off some steam to get rid of the rage that had been building up inside of him for the past few years. Some of Brett's friends had warned him months ago that she was cheating on him with someone at the tennis club or the gym at the hotel she had as part of her membership. Maybe the strikingly handsome tennis coach or some pumped steroid-ridden iron man who was probably ten years younger than Cheryl who saw her as another notch on his belt. But instead of being angry and confronting her, he just felt relief and it just made his future plans and life a lot easier. Whoever it was, is welcome to have her, and I hope they have deep pockets to support her lifestyle. In any event, they would soon send her packing after a week or so. She was far too complicated and irritating.

Brett suspected Cheryl had been cheating on him for years with different men, he even suspected one of them was an office colleague or possibly a friend of his but he didn't care. Cheryl always had hold of her phone, and the landline would ring at strange times of the day and sometimes in late evenings, and when he answered the call it then mysteriously cut off. He suspected it might be the wife or girlfriend of one of her lovers who wanted to tell him the truth or maybe another man, he really wasn't bothered at all. Many times he just wanted to scream down the phone, "Whoever you are, have her, please take her off my hands." Cheryl really must have thought so little of him, how stupid he was, he had to do something quick, he had to leave her and soon before he committed some act of gross vengeance out of mere frustration but then again Cheryl knew that wasn't in Brett's nature.

He feared she might even use this further to her advantage. The prospect of perhaps more extreme mental abuse from her sent cold shivers down his spine and he was certainly not prepared to sit tight and wait for this to evolve.

The next morning, Freya could think of nothing else but starting afresh, somewhere new, somewhere peaceful and quiet to gather her thoughts and hopefully turn her life around. She always thought of that childhood holiday on a Greek island, their one and only holiday as a family (when Pops was alive), a memory she had treasured, a happy place.

She and her sister Daisy were very young at the time but Freya remembered where little old ladies dressed in black clothing sat outside their homes, where the grapes grew freely on trees. The times walking with Pops through those narrow-cobbled streets looking longingly at the bright, paint-washed Fisherman's cottages glistening in the warm spring sunshine as he reached up to the overhanging branches plucking handfuls of the ripened grapes and pushed them into their opened hands for them to instantly eat, not saving a one for him.

They tasted beautiful and sweet and had no resemblance to the pre-packed ones sold in large supermarkets, after all, these were organic and nature's best. She recalled the stories he told during these walks, stories that made them both laugh and she was sure there were parts in them that were exaggerated but they were nonetheless happy memories. Possibly, those happier days, as she remembered them, gave her thoughts of returning to that beautiful island and she wanted to go there again to remember happy times, to remember Pops. Perhaps this was the very chance for her to get back control of her life and banish those negative thoughts that gripped her very soul. All her life, she had spent looking in search of happiness and had never found it (she thought Nick would be that person; a husband, lover and soulmate).

What was she doing wrong? She sure as hell didn't want to end up like her drunken, drug-addled mother or, worse, become a total recluse.

Freya was kind, hardworking, and attractive, yet real love had always eluded her, including, as it turned out, Nick! She had nothing left; he had taken that with him and left her with a broken heart. Now there was no husband, no children, a career he had manufactured, one she completely hated, and no explanation for why, having arrived home one day, he had gone.

Dissipated into thin air; no note, no phone call or text message, nothing—whoosh like a puff of smoke as if he never existed (what an idiot she was).

While she was working and trying to build a life for them, he was secretly gambling, lying, cheating, and fraudulently stealing money from his clients' accounts to support his habits. Did he buy drugs too? She had noticed strange behavioural patterns appearing some months before he left, something she had never witnessed from him before. Was he snorting cocaine? It certainly might explain his bizarre mood changes. The stockbroker partners with whom he worked were never able to trace the money or him, and they were mortified to know how the hell he managed to extract large sums in such a short space of time, unnoticed and without being able to account for the transfers. He had somehow overridden the fall-back security systems and bridged the banking files, but then again, he was a very clever thief and an even more accomplished conman! Just exactly how much money he had stolen Freya was unable to find out; the senior partners were very tight-lipped as it had now become a police matter and was being investigated by the serious crime unit at the Met Office in London.

She herself had been interviewed by some detective inspector and his sidekick, but she realised she was an innocent part of the whole sorry situation. They even felt sorry for her, but at the time, it was a small comfort.

She now had little money to support herself along with the continuous gossip-mongers who understandably thought she was his mule and must have known what Nick was doing. He had gambled everything in their lives; their love, nearly their home, her good reputation, emptied their joint bank account and then disappeared on the arm of another fool-smitten floozy, or some bimbo client he was swindling money from. Who knows just where he'll show up next, certainly not the UK as there was a warrant out for his arrest and was now classified as a serious criminal on the run.

"Do it, Freya," she said to herself, "it's make or break time, just follow your dream." The distress and embarrassment of it all had almost broken her; some bits were blocked by the booze for a while. The mornings were always the worst; so many mornings Freya woke sprawled on the floor surrounded by empty bottles, it was just too painful to be sober, she needed that one last drink to kill the pain. It started with one glass which became two, three became four and then the bottle had been consumed all in less than an hour. Another screw top immediately undone, bottle number two just as quickly and easily drunk, the taste gone in a flash. Pinot Grigio's 'Three for a Tenner' from the local Spar; after all, it matched her budget; quantity over quality!

Friends came and left, some to have a drink, others to check on her, but she found their help and advice just an unwelcome intrusion.

Although, in reality, some of them did try to talk some sense into her, but they eventually gave up on her booze-ridden bedraggled face and obsessed self-pity. To her, it felt worse than grief and it was hers to wallow in. Several weeks followed and slowly, her close friends left and didn't make contact with her. No 'WhatsApp' messages and deleted her from their social media accounts.

"All just like Nick," she said. "I don't need him and I don't need them." Loosening another screw cap. She felt betrayed and lonely and it was only months later after she found the strength to quit the booze when suddenly she was able to see through the foggy mist of the evaporating alcohol, she realised they had actually done her a favour. Leaving her to squander in self-pity, she wasn't dying, she had a life to live, it was up to her which road she wanted to take, the road to despair or the avenue of dreams. Freya chose the latter, and the belief in following those dreams is what saved her. The bottle would have eventually killed her and stripped her of whatever dignity she had. She was beginning to follow the same path as her mother but she owed it to her sister Daisy more than that, and indeed to herself. God forbid if she became a mirror and emulated her mother. The very thought brought all over shivers just like someone had walked over her grave.

Freya eventually understood the meaning of why some people go down the road of despair, and lose all hope. And how easy it is to pick up a bottle to kill the pain, to kill the tragedies in life, how easy to hide behind a bottle, a bottle that never stops, never gets empty and then eventually it is too late to stop. It takes over. It made Freya sad to think some people don't have the inner strength or mental energy to stop and find the support they need.

They must feel so helpless and alone. Freya knew it was sometimes the blows in life that take you down the wrong path and change that person. Freya wanted to be a different person and she had the mindset to do that and wanted to help others. But this was to be her turn but first, she needed some time out to find herself again and evaluate life's journey.

Nick had never tried to make contact with her and she had heard through the grapevine that he was on the Interpol record file for fraud and money laundering. The very thought sickened her to the stomach; to think some poor vulnerable person had been robbed of their life savings and investments for Nick's so-called early retirement plans, taken to the cleaners by her ex-husband to fund a lifestyle that was never possible on his basic income. If he ever came back into the country, he would end up behind bars and that is what had been said to her by the detective inspector.

She was glad, following their long questioning of her she had finally convinced them she had no idea what Nick had been doing. It transpired during those conducted interviews, he had a police file as long as your arm, from petty theft to robbery fraud and even attempted rape. Freya had, through social media channels, managed to contact the woman Nick had allegedly tried to rape. The details of those events were truly shocking. The woman wished to remain anonymous and for her own reasons never proceeded with the claim, a trial was the last thing she needed to go through. She also feared for her safety, scared of what may happen to her, and now she had a new life, a devoted loving husband who was unaware of past events and a baby on the way.

She didn't have the mental strength to delve into the past; for her family and all and sundry to share her ordeal. It was to remain a closed book, she just wanted to move on and deal with more important priorities. Freya completely understood and gave long thoughts on why so many women or men never reported abuse or rape claims. Was it just too hard for them to have to go through the ordeal again in an open court like the hanging out of dirty washing? It sickened her that Nick and she had shared a bed together and he yet again escaped justice. What a completely out-and-out utter 'b*****d!'

The police were convinced he would slip up one day; sitting around a ram-shackled out-of-the-way beach bar in Rio or some far East village gossiping with the locals, bragging about his exploits. Even the underworld sometimes gives up criminals for their own protection and anonymity. He would ultimately pay for his crimes they were sure of that, but that didn't dissolve the hurt and shame she felt inside. At first, Freya became paranoid and thought people were pointing the finger at her. "You cannot tell me she didn't know." She overheard some of the staff whispering at work and they were right, maybe she would have said the same if it wasn't her it had happened to. But she was unable to change where the situation ended or began to unravel.

Of all the people in the world, she had to go and fall in love with a full-blown aptly named 'Dirty John' for all the consequences that came with it she'd bought the 'T'-shirt, been awarded the trophy with a big pile of horse manure on top for good measure. She prayed that one day he'd make another mistake and he would fall flat on his rotten-to-the-core face and boy; she would love to be around when it happened.

Freya once tried to contact Nick's parents, whom she had never met. Nick said he had no family, that his maternal parents had died when he was young, that he had been adopted at the age of five, and that they too had recently passed away.

He had no siblings, aunts, uncles, or cousins that he had been made aware of, and growing up for him was extremely lonely. He admitted to being a loner with few friends, which was confirmed at their wedding ceremony at the registry office when there were just the two of them and a witness brought from outside the registry office. A rather plain and unflattering service; but then Nick was so convincing, and when you love someone and you have no reason to question it, why would you? Freya also had the same story, only hers was not a lie; her mother was dead to her. Nick had never met her mother or sister, Daisy; it was just easier that way; no one wants to drag up the past, which is why there was simply no conversation of our families, and he maintained that going forward it wasn't beneficial. After he had left, there was just one occasion when, merely out of curiosity, Freya began browsing the internet through the usual social media sites, and by a freak chance, she discovered what she thought was a mobile number for Nick's parents. Out of boredom or perhaps even desperation, she spent hours, days, and weeks chasing the preverbal needle in a haystack and left no stone unturned. She persevered and kept on searching, and finally, some truth came from Nick: his adopted parents had passed away sadly two years prior to them meeting in tragic circumstances at a house fire. But his web of deceit continued as his maternal and biological family were well and truly alive. Freya called the number she had discovered several times and hoped that it was them.

She left numerous voicemails, and for a week or so, there was no answer or response, not even a message of any kind. Then suddenly, one afternoon, some weeks later, the phone rang. It was an unknown number with no caller ID. She was reluctant to answer an unknown number as it was always a stupid answer machine, some annoying salesperson, the usual (we believe you were involved in an accident last year), or someone trying to steal your hard-earned savings. But only through some morbid curiosity or intuition, this time she answered without giving it a second thought. "Hello," said Freya, "who is this?" A very soft-spoken woman replied, "Forget about him, my love, me and his late father did a long time ago, he is a deeply troubled soul, evil to the core, he has the devil's blood running through him, you really should move on with your life, trust me when I say this you've had a lucky and extremely narrow escape. Please never try to contact me again some things are best forgotten I have no wish to know further about you or the troubles he has brought on you, the stress and upset of his continuous dodgy dealings are what killed his late father. I will be deleting and blocking your number." And with that she abruptly hung up, never giving Freya the right to reply.

Freya also deleted the number and made it her bond not to make any further contact again. She was now too frightened to know about those early chapters of Nick's life and what avenues it would take her and she did not want to know given the bizarre conversation albeit one way she had just had with his mother. Yet intriguingly and strangely, Freya was still curious of what was the reason for his mother to give up her child for adoption at such a very young age and why she trembled at the mere mention of her son's name.

There was more to come from Nick she knew and felt it, but it was too horrifying to think about, one day the truth may come out, she really did not want to know anymore, she had no intention of delving further into his murky past, Sarah's Law or not let sleeping dogs lie. The harsh words from his mother convinced her to leave well alone. Freya eventually settled in bed but had a disturbed and fretful night's sleep; all this now was getting too much and beyond her control. The past few hours convinced her she simply needed to get away, anywhere for the sake of her own sanity and bloody well soon!

It was a cold, damp, autumn Tuesday morning; Brett arrived at work unusually late as the train decided too many leaves on the track. Pulling up his chair passing the same few staff who meaningfully hollered, "Morning, Boss, see it's pissing down again."

Adam, a senior partner in the business was for once annoyingly on time as lateness would be the opening title at the top of his CV. Adam made some cheap remark about punctuality being the courtesy of kings! But then it sounded crass and unnecessary, no one laughed. The sarcastic tone had rebounded on Adam as the entire office remained silent. He shuffled off to the tea room keeping his head down shouting loudly, "Coffee, anyone?" Brett looked at the same papers which had now been on his desk since last Thursday. How boring, boring, boring. He really could not 'give a rat's' anymore. They had recently moved into new offices just a few weeks earlier; although they were slightly smaller, they were only a block away on the next street and the rent was significantly cheaper.

In fairness to Adam, he was an excellent networker, bringing in many new clients and due to his vast array of resources managed to secure a great deal. This is what made him the perfect business partner and a huge asset in sharing the workload. He was also really good at his job, eight years younger than Brett but had the same sharpness and was very ambitious, which is why Brett awarded him his directorship last year. Keep him, sweet, don't lose him, he was too invaluable. Yet everything else for Brett these days was just the same, he was so fed up now and needed to be motivated.

Right now he was so far from it; he had lost concentration and focus, his mind was not on the job it was somewhere else, always to the same place to a woman he loved but didn't know, chasing a dream, it had now become an obsession. He hoped Adam or any of the other staff hadn't noticed this distraction or reflected in his share of the work rota. But it was for Brett, 'angel' was always there in his head constantly in his mind and try as he might he could not stop it. His mother was right. "It's never too late to change, make the move, Brett." The words bellowed through his brain, he had to make it happen he was going to make his mother proud.

"That is it," Brett said loudly (a bit too loudly, he thought), the others in the office were staring at him now, time to think about yourself for once, stand up, be a man, take charge, after all, what did he have to lose. He threw back his head and sitting at his neat and tidy desk he just stared into space thinking now of how to plan his next move, the next step, the next chapter in his life. It would make a good book. Brett laughed to himself.

He was rudely jolted back from drifting into the abyss when the telephone rang. It was Cheryl. "What now?" he muttered reluctantly taking the call.

"Hurry home tonight, darling, don't be late, finish early as I need you to call in on your way home at that delightful boutique wine shop in the village and ask them to deliver twenty-four bottles of their finest mix of red and whites tomorrow morning.

And ask them to include a couple of bottles of Champers. Oh, and bring a couple of bottles with you for me to sample tonight at dinner and, Brett darling, don't be cheap, you know I hate cheapness (or as you're always saying value). Well, on this occasion, I don't want value, or stress to their quality or it'll go back, I'm throwing a dinner party tomorrow evening." Brett barely managed to get a word in before as quickly as she spoke, she hung up on him. He never got the opportunity for her explanation of who exactly the party was for and why. Some new near neighbour no doubt; any excuse to show off. What he did know it wouldn't be for him.

"Cheryl, Cheryl, bloody Cheryl." Life for her always revolved around Cheryl. He loved her and hated her in so many different ways, even more now, he needed to get away and follow his dreams without Cheryl and to his 'angel' and tonight he would get the party well and truly started, he was going to put his foot down and tell her, dinner party or not, it was going to be showdown time at the Ok Corral!

He was completely sick of her now, her demanding ways, how she patronised and humiliated him in front of others. It was just materialistic for Cheryl, who had the best house, who threw the best parties, it was so bloody boring to hear. He started to dislike her even more.

Had he made her this way by giving in, and should he have taken control early in the marriage instead of giving in to her every whim or request? Brett knew he had to because he could never give her the children she desired.

Within the first year, he asked her to leave him and find someone else, but she wouldn't; she said she loved him too much and they had each other; that was all that mattered; they didn't need children. "Brett, I love you; we can be happy, I promise you, and one day we can, considering adoption, give a child a loving home." That never happened, and as time passed, things changed, and so did Cheryl.

While many of her friends were having babies and settling into family life, things got harder, and he continued to give her anything she wanted, except the one thing she craved most in her life: 'children'. It became tough for him. Cheryl became more bitter and demanding. She moved back home with her parents for a while; Brett had encouraged her, but she didn't stay too long as her parents couldn't cope with her overly demanding ways. It was too much for them to bear putting pressure on her to leave Brett, as they believed it was his fault for how much worse Cheryl had become and for failing them by not providing them with grandchildren of their own. They made their thoughts known to Brett and exactly how they resented him. They made it abundantly clear who at fault—him!

He despised them and now realised just why Cheryl had become a mirror of them. He could never imagine that if he had had the opportunity to have kids, he would ever bring them up to behave in their selfish ways.

Cheryl, their own daughter, was spoiled, self-conceited, patronising, and the most uncaring person he'd ever come across, and what made it worse was that she was his wife... for now!

He was sure their few friends thought the same, but they would never say anything. Some of Brett's friends made jokes about her in a meaningful way but were careful not to hurt his feelings. They had seen a change in Brett over the years and it saddened them; they were just thankful Cheryl did not belong to any of them. Yes, she was great to look at and had a tremendous figure, but that is where it ended, and to be honest, they were all perhaps a tad intimidated by her. Combined with that vicious tongue of hers, she could put you back in your place with the snap of her fingers, and so they trod carefully around her for fear of breaking the eggshells. They suspected she was cheating on Brett but said nothing; it was just the best thing to do in the circumstances; he had to figure it out for himself. They knew Brett was far too good for her; he was better-natured and much more classy than Cheryl.

Brett had often spoken to Ben, one of his closest friends, the one he could trust the most, he told him about the move he wanted to make, his childhood dream (for obvious reasons he didn't mention angel), Ben was with him all the way.

"Do it mate, get out of here if it's killing you and please if I can help ask me, I promise to keep this to ourselves just go for it whilst you can and before you change your mind."

And so tonight it was Brett's chance, he was silently terrified of the fallout that was about to unfold but the adrenalin rushing through his body almost excited him.

Usually, Brett walked to the train station after work, it helped him relax and he usually got there early to have a quick pint in the platform bar before he got on the train. But today was going to be different. He jumped in a taxi to the station to get an earlier train as Cheryl had told him to do but he was not visiting the wine shop as again Cheryl had demanded he did, he was heading home post haste in readiness for the confrontation. He just wanted it over and done with, to get the ball rolling. Luckily, there was a taxi pulling up outside the office looking for a fare and settling in the back seat he couldn't help in hearing the radio perhaps a little too loud for his liking, but it was the Eagles one of his favourite groups and so on this occasion he didn't mind.

Brett sniggered to himself, ironically, the track playing was 'Fabulous' the words rang so true, 'You were just too busy being fabulous to think about us' and those words were certainly the hallmarks that was Cheryl. Just maybe this was a sign giving him the confidence that this was going to happen. For sure, it was too late to go back now.

Brett arrived home. Cheryl was on the phone as per usual nothing new he thought, there was not even a 'hello, how are you, my love, peck on the cheek sort of welcome', not an acknowledgement he was in the house (was he expecting that? When was the last time that happened?). It was then she noticed Brett hadn't brought any wine. At this, she swiftly interrupted her call, whoever it was they were clearly not that important and clutching the receiver under her chin peering annoyingly over her designer glasses she blurted out in her usual patronising tone, "Where the bloody hell is my wine?"

Brett immediately responded, "I'm leaving. I damn well know you are snapped, Cheryl," leaving this very minute to get the wine.

"I give you one small job to pick up wine and you stand in front of me empty-handed. For god's sake, Brett."

"Don't you dare remove your coat; I need you to leave for the village wine merchants right this minute. That was the one simple task I asked of you, the caterers have everything else in hand for tomorrow so just GO!"

"I'm leaving," Brett said louder and in a firmer tone.

"I heard you the first time," she yelled, "and so can Maureen on the telephone."

"Good," he yelled louder, "it's you, Cheryl, I'm leaving YOU, we're done, it's over. I am out of here asap." He wanted to stay and give her a real piece of his mind and shout obscenities at her but resisted, out of self-respect he wanted to do things in a dignified way and that would just delay the matter ahead. Cheryl by now had covered the earpiece with her hand so Maureen could not hear.

"What the hell," she yelled, and with that Brett picked up his pre-prepared holdall from his office in the hallway and turned to walk away. He quietly smiled congratulating himself as he knew that Mount Vesuvius was about to erupt any time soon. And so it did! All hell broke loose that evening, no way was Cheryl going anywhere and neither was he. "What about my friends?" she screamed. "My drama classes, my evenings out and my life with you?"

Brett replied, "I have no life, Cheryl, I just exist and I cannot and will not take anymore. I want us both to be happy."

"I've sacrificed everything for you god damn it," she screamed. "You could not give me children when I could have had any man I wanted and you tell me you are leaving. I'll be damned if I am going anywhere and neither are you. I cannot understand you," she wailed.

"What in hell's name is wrong with you? You have everything here and most of all me. You're just having a bad day, darling, a mid-life crisis, it happens and it will pass."

She clearly just didn't get it, Brett thought, she still was only thinking about herself again and this made him even more angry, she even brought up her trump card (children) what a bitch. He had married the devil incarnate and she was getting worse every day. It was now or never, it really was time to go, he knew what he had to do and he also knew just how much more bitter and selfish Cheryl had become. Deep down Brett recognised how she wished she had left him in the early days and had the children she so desired. Cheryl was far too self-centred now for her to leave him for another man who could give her children. She was far too egotistical and in any event, she would probably raise her child a monster like her and that would not be fair on any child to be the mirror image of their parent's ways. And with that, he closed the front porch door firmly behind him.

Freya arrived home, as usual, these past months, unhappy. It would have been hard to paint a smile on her face. She was lonely, so very lonely and no one seemed to notice. While others were continuing building their lives, Freya was crumbling, she felt alone.

Right now she needed a holiday to get away somewhere she didn't want to hide anymore, her mind was made up and nothing or no one was going to stop her. Never again would she feel so lonely and afraid of the world and what she had been dealt with.

Following those few therapy sessions with Dr Alled, Freya realised she was not alone and that there were other people in her situation and some much worse. Dr Alled had suggested a break, a holiday, spend time with family. The latter was off the cards, especially with her mother.

That was an avenue too far right now and for her own sanity, she kept her distance. Her mother was a complete bitch anyway and had been with Freya for most of her life favouring her sister Daisy more. She was a troubled woman who favoured male attention over her own kids and both their childhoods had been unpleasant and troubling, to say the least. Men coming and going at all times, different dads or as mum said they had to call them. They never lasted, they left after a while and she was left to look after Daisy while Mother became more objectionable and drank bottle after bottle after bottle consuming anything that resembled a quick brain-numbing fix. Poor Daisy was so fragile she had on a couple of occasions tried to commit suicide, fortunately unsuccessfully. Freya tried so hard to talk to Daisy but she never spoke much as she was a shy kid, she dressed differently from others and she lived in her own little world.

Who could blame her as there was enough going on in their shitty childhood, anyway probably was best for her to keep her head down but Freya couldn't help but worry about Daisy, something was not right and it began to trouble her.

Sadly, when 'Pops' died their childhood became about survival and finding ways how to leave home as soon as they could. Daisy was three years and seven months younger than

Freya and she needed lots of attention and looking after and when Poppa Jeff passed away it just got worse, they missed him so much he was their rock, the person they turned to first for advice.

Poppa Jeff gave so much reassurance to them whilst he took anything and everything derogatory and unkind from their mother.

He always remained dignified, well at least in front of them probably, for their protection, he was always there. Their mother was a drunk and they often wondered how their father put up with it but he did and their childhood was good when Pops was around, but when he died that was when life got tough causing poor Daisy to regress and sink into deep depression. Freya was out most nights either working at the local diner trying hard to save up enough money so she and Daisy could find a place of their own and into a more peaceful situation. They needed money to eat and live.

Occasionally, the owner of the diner let Freya make up take-home boxes from food that was about to be past use by, he knew of her home circumstances and that there was barely food at home for her. He enquired many times with Freya learning from her home was just a fridge full of booze and dirty ashtrays everywhere, the house stank like a brothel and was fast becoming one. Daisy often begged to go with Freya, "Please don't leave me here, Freya, I hate it so much let me come to work with you please!"

"I'm sorry, Daisy, the boss is really good to me and I can't be making him responsible for you, it's not fair for him and I don't want to lose my job it's our only way out right now. You have to stay you're too young to hang around with me, stay in your room keep your head down and study hard. Daisy, you need to get good grades so you can go to college anyway Mum will not even notice you're home. Lock your door keep out of her way and I will bring takeaway food home for us both when I've finished work."

It broke Freya's heart to leave Daisy so upset but she had to for both their sakes. More so as Mother was 'always away with the fairies', and in no fit condition physically or mentally to look after her own kids. All the time men and women were coming and going like ships in the night.

Their family had now become hot gossip, the 'talk of the town', close neighbours looking at them with disdain and total disgust at the way Mother was behaving reflecting on Daisy and Freya very badly. It was too awful for them to bear.

They often found Mother sprawled on the floor, sometimes laying in her own vomit, the occasional black eye or blooded lip from a fall or a fight, male or female she was always up for it and never backed down. She was an utter disgrace and Freya treated her with contempt and disgust, but it was their mother after all so she picked her up cleaned whatever mess was waiting and tried very hard to remain patient particularly as this had become the regular pattern day after day. There was to be no let-up. Freya couldn't believe how her mother kept a job let alone maintain a roof over their heads but somehow, she did. It had been said she was regularly sleeping with her boss maybe that had something to do with it. Everything in the house smelt of cigarettes and stale booze; it was unkempt and a total shambles, to say the least but Mother being Mother always looked immaculate when she left the house however quite she managed it was a mystery but it worked for her. The major concern for Freya was that someday it would all come crashing down leaving her and Daisy in the crossfire. It would be nothing more than she deserved. She treated them shabbily.

Heartlessly, Freya felt everything that was coming to her mother was solely of her own making and out of their control. She just needed to get her and Daisy away quickly before the walls came tumbling in.

It had never always been like this she had never been a good mother, to say the least, but in their younger days, you might just get a little hug out of her if you were lucky. But when Pops died, her kids became a burden and she never acknowledged they were around and as far as Freya was concerned their mother had put their father in an early grave. She regularly treated him like something the cat had brought in, she cheated, she flirted, she was blatantly unfaithful and lied constantly to him. Freya had witnessed this on many occasions. Different men were coming and going while Dad was working. Freya wasn't stupid it wasn't the rent or gas man, she was disgusted with her mother and kept it her secret she thought it would destroy Pops and any love he had for her and Daisy. It would break his heart knowing the truth, and what if he left home leaving them to fend for themselves? She wasn't prepared to take that risk, she felt immensely guilty but she and Daisy needed and loved their dad so much. As a consequence, Freya lied for their sake, hers and Daisy and the very thought of what she felt she had to do all the years ago still haunts her to this very day. Freya knew Mother maintained her secret and that is why she favoured Daisy.

Freya didn't accept the guilt and shame her mother had brought to herself and felt the death of Pops was inevitable.

Mother was too embarrassed to even look at them at Poppa Jeff's funeral, she never wept and kept her gaunt face gazing uncaringly down towards the floor.

Mother would now have to fend for herself just as she and Daisy had to and that is precisely what she did live her life as if they never existed. Freya just once managed to get a glimpse of her mother's eye at the funeral for what seemed to be a few seconds barely a glimpse or so of comfort. And that is when she knew she and Daisy were in for a rough few years ahead. The very thoughts petrified the hell out of her but do it she would for Pops, she would make him proud and, in the process, make sure her and Daisy came out of this with recognition and better to face the next journey in life. Working hard at the diner and with the help of a raise and bonuses from the owner she was able to save up enough money for a deposit to rent a room from a friend. It wasn't a huge space but cosy, warm and homely with just enough room for the two of them. It enabled Daisy to come and go as she pleased even if it meant one of them sleeping on the 'put up' on the floor.

Daisy did her very level best in keeping out of Mother's harmful ways, keeping her head down until the day she would get the hell away from there to a good college as far away as possible.

Amazingly, despite all the constant distractions, Daisy studied really hard, burying her head in her study books on every occasion eventually achieving excellent grades. She received an offer and accepted to study for a higher national degree at a well-renowned college for art and design that hopefully would in the future bring her recognition and great success. Daisy saw this as the perfect opportunity to be away from Mother's toxic environment far away and a far greater possibility to form her own character and independence 'a fresh start in life'.

Freya was so proud of her, she was a great sister and Pops would have been so proud of her too it brought tears to her eyes. Daisy was finally a free spirit free to spread her wings now they had both left their mother's appalling bubble for good. The woman was now alone to dwell in self-pity with no one to pick up the pieces she cried and screamed like a lost child when Freya finally picked up the last of Daisy's belongings. Freya looked at her mother in disgust and quietly closed the door behind her and she knew this would be the last time she would ever see her again. She felt nothing. Daisy was now on the mend, on the road to recovery. She kept in touch with Freya with letters never any phone calls, it must have been easier for Daisy to put down words in letters and that was fine for Freya as long as she knew she was okay, that was all that mattered to her.

And that's how it remained for a few years they both just moved on with their lives, but Daisy had memories that would haunt her forever and Freya was about to find out the truth.

Daisy was on the mend she explained in her last letter and had found love and compassion with a woman called Mary and it was working for her. She was ultimately, ecstatically happy. Freya didn't want to contact her and turn her life upside down and open old wounds. She didn't speak much and Freya often wondered if one of her mother's lovers had ever touched Daisy or even worse. She couldn't go there. Maybe one day Daisy would find the strength to talk to her. Freya was just happy to know she had a good partner in Mary and she was finally moving on with her life. Mother on the other hand hadn't and Freya certainly did not want to be like her if their father had survived things may have been different, but who knows what the future would hold.

She had witnessed that first hand, got the medal, the t-shirt and the other crap thrown in for good measure. Yet deep down Freya could feel the tug in her heart that someone was waiting for her, and a hope someone wanted her, she had to discover that for her own sanity.

Brett slept alone that night. As soon as he closed his eyes 'angel' was calling for him and for the first time thought he saw her smile. A tear fell softly down his cheek!

He knew he had made the right decision it was time to go, to find his future even if that meant being alone, after all, hadn't he felt alone for many years in his marriage, how much worse could it get? He could only recall a handful of times when he was happy, he laughed to himself. He remembered their wedding day; Cheryl looked stunning and beautifully radiant, how lucky he thought he was back then and he could still see his mother's face as if it was yesterday, she was trying to smile for Brett's sake; he laughed again it was funny how he could see that now. He should have run, his mother was right but it was Brett's mistake and now he was taking positive action. The next few months were the saddest and hardest he had to endure. Saying goodbye to Mum, close friends and work colleagues; it wasn't a surprise when Brett's friends said, "You should have left sooner, mate, how the hell you have put up with it for so long." The thoughts of 'angel' had kept him strong, always there in his mind and heart; she was the only one he could not say goodbye to; she kept him from going totally insane (if only she was real).

Cheryl had not spoken to him for the whole time, she was astonished her Brett was leaving her, she would be the talk of the town, how could he do this to her?

Brett didn't seem to care anymore he knew she would move on, find someone else, she probably had already; she was still young enough to start again and maybe even have the family she so desired.

He did not want to fight her anymore, he had to be happy and Cheryl was not doing that for him. She would move on in time who knows and at this moment who cares. Brett and Cheryl lived separate lives over the next months. Brett spent time between Greece and the odd hotel room and occasionally at home. It was hard living under the same roof but then Cheryl made it that way. He had to persevere, moving to another country was going to take considerable time and he was not giving in now, he had come too far now to go back. He continued to visit his mother as often as he could. Vivienne herself had found some renewed excitement and vigour. She encouraged Brett enormously and now that he had made the decision, he was to see it through.

"Don't go back, Son," she said, "make sure you have that mental energy to continue in your quest for happiness."

Brett had managed to convince Adam to buy his share of the business and those arrangements gave Brett some of the funds he needed for the move to Greece. He had also saved the small legacy from his father's will, and a generous gift from his mother gave him the financial resources needed. He spent considerable time, energy and money on his new home and vineyard but whilst progress was slower than anticipated he was delighted how the project he began some months earlier was at long last taking shape.

He could now visualise the end result and he silently complimented himself, but after all his profession as a quantity surveyor helped enormously.

He was excited and nervous and could not believe it was at long last coming together. It was a big move for him and if things had turned out differently in their marriage it could have worked (well maybe) it was never Cheryl's dream they were two different souls who should never have met let alone marry. Brett giggled he almost felt like a teenager again. He asked for very little of Cheryl only what he was entitled to and tried to keep it as amicable as possible. It wasn't easy. Cheryl threw several tantrums she continually failed to recognise what was happening almost in shock, but as soon as it took to talking of finances she bolted back into the reality of the situation. Brett always remained polite and considerate after all it was him that had burst her vacuous world. He suggested more out of guilt that once all was completed, she would be free to come over to Greece and spend some time, bring a friend too if you wish. He knew that would never happen, clearly, Cheryl had made him aware that at this moment and going forward how much she loathed him for doing this to her. The woman scorned was the card being played! Once work permits and visas had been fully implemented and he had made the permanent move to Greece it was highly unlikely he would hear from Cheryl again.

No doubt any future contact would be through her solicitors (Goss and Turner LLP) who advised her to avoid court proceedings and they would negotiate directly with Brett on her behalf rather than drag it out for months or years. It proved good simple advice, and despite the toughness of negotiating with Simon Turner, he found them to be realistic, after all, they were acting for Cheryl on a fixed fee basis so it was in their best interests not to prolong the outcome.

Lives change, people change, you just have to close the door behind you and lock it. Life's a hurdle, you keep running until you get to where you want to be, once you are there you pause and draw breath. Brett anticipated the Greek Island dream would be his final destination. He loved the place so much and it wasn't too far away from where he and his parents had visited on numerous occasions in his childhood years, they were always lovely happy memories and he always vowed to return later in life. Brett had travelled to different places with Cheryl in the past, yet nothing came close to Greece; the love he had for this country; something always pulled him back there. Brett remembered the special times he had with his parents and it made him happy. Very happy, and soon his dream would become a reality.

Freya was a tad nervous, a holiday alone, who would have believed it, she thought, having the courage, me, 'Freya Johnson' travelling alone.

She always had a deadbeat of a boyfriend or Nick reluctantly tagging along, they weren't very memorable and it always ended in disaster or fallouts! "You are running away again," her friends mocked, but what did they know, they did not really know her at all. Never mind them, she thought, I deserve some happiness. They were never really there when she needed them most; when her life was crumbling and she was desperately trying to not lose her home. Where were they then, when she cried herself to sleep each night reaching out for someone to help? Those days were the loneliest and hardest times she ever had to endure, they never knew her pain, the hardship, and she hoped they would never experience any of that.

But, hey, life does not always go to plan and she knew it first-hand and had somehow managed to survive. She was now ready to make her next step in life.

"Be a big girl, an adult," she said to herself, "you have done it in the past and can do it again." But why was she so scared, it was just a holiday. She had been through much worse when 'Pops' died; what could possibly go wrong?

As the plane touched down Freya felt alive, and relieved, everything felt real and so beautiful what had she been doing all her life? All the unhappiness and gloom evaporated immediately the moment she disembarked the plane as she put that first foot on the airport Tarmac. She was reborn.

The next few days she spent walking, absorbing the crisp spring sunshine and thinking things through. Just how different life seems when you take yourself away from unpleasant and intolerable situations, she wanted to stay here forever and never leave. She had nothing to lose; who would miss her? No one she thought. She could take a sabbatical from her job for a few months, there was nothing urgent or spoiling, her new boss 'Cheryl' (who was a bit of a tyrant with the staff somehow had taken a shine to Freya) and was very understanding as she herself had recently been through a rather unhappy and unpleasant 'breakup'. Freya started to believe it was possible and was convinced she had to give it a try. Besides, there was plenty of work here, mostly bar work or domestic help jobs. She was not afraid to put her hand on anything and knew she needed to be flexible to make this happen. It wasn't impossible and would find something to tie her over until at least she re-evaluated her situation, a penultimate decision at first before taking that final step. It would have to be one that suited her, and not anyone else. Freya was going to ask work if she could take a couple of months of unpaid leave just to give her time to fully reflect and in the process rediscover herself once more.

"No knee-jerk reactions now," she said, "be positive and think this through."

Having chatted to the owner of the studio apartment, she had initially taken for her two-week holiday, he told her it would be available on a short-term lease and at a discounted price. He had offered her a good deal, one too good to turn down. The local people were so warm and friendly and this helped her make the decision to stay, her mind was made up, let's give it a go! Yet there was something else drawing her to stay, some kind of magnetic force was keeping her here, was that possible, she thought, or am I just being delusional.

Freya finally plucked up the courage to call Daisy and was able to convince her sister that they should talk as for her the stage in the healing process had now been reached. That evening from her small studio apartment, she felt a strong need to speak to her sister, a cloud, a nagging doubt over her head had doubted her far too long now and it was this that Freya needed to clear the air. Freya spoke first asking Daisy if was she free to talk, Daisy answered with a cheerful voice, "Is that you, Freya? Yes, I'm fine thanks all is good." It cheered Freya up to hear her sisters' voice and how happy she sounded. They chatted for a while filling each other in on past events. Freya was shocked when Daisy told her something she had been dreading hearing for many years, (Dad) Dave as they were meant to call him had been visiting Daisy's room on many occasions.

Mother knew what was happening and completely failed to stop or deal with it.

How very inhumane and disgusting a parent could let this happen to an underage child in their care. Freya felt an instant repulsiveness and anger at how their mother had failed in her duty to protect Daisy.

"Oh, my little baby sister, I'm so sorry, why didn't you tell me, I could have helped you."

"I was not ready," replied Daisy. "I believed it wasn't happening to me. I felt dirty, Freya, and that is why Mother treated me nice and bought me presents. It was meant to soften the pain, to keep me quiet and cover up her guilt." Freya felt the anger erupt inside her once more, how she could ever find it in her heart to forgive that woman? Why did she let this happen to her child, as a mother your instincts are to protect your children, she was a disgraceful adult and so-called parent.

"Daisy, sweetheart, please forgive me, I should have protected you more, please forgive me." Freya sobbed so hard she felt her heart crumbling and she was now utterly distraught by what had happened to Daisy.

Daisy answered, "You were not to know, Freya, I kept it to myself as self-protection, it was Mother that has let us both down, we were both kids for heaven's sake we practically brought ourselves up after Poppa Jeff died, we had no choice. But we do know now, we cannot change the past but we are both free and can change our futures, our destinies.

"Look at you alone in another country, not afraid to restart, we survived and no worse from the ordeals we faced, stronger too, Freya, you must follow your heart the rest will fall into place, who knows what path it will take for you, my darling sister, I love so much." And with that, they hung up the phone.

After another long heartfelt chat, Daisy told Freya she was taking legal action and to not worry as her partner Mary was in total and full support, with her all the way. She would keep Freya updated on all developments as they happened and would call her more often. Freya put down the phone and found it hard not to call Mother and give her a dressing down and what for 'what a bitch' but Daisy pleaded with her not to make that call as it would make matters worse and it could be used against them as witness tampering. Daisy would get her day in court with Mother and that dirty bastard Dave, the so-called 'dad' who had abused her for all those years. Freya agreed she would be there too, the disgusting pair deserved everything that was coming to them, poor Daisy. All those years and she knew nothing. If she wasn't there for her then she certainly would be now. She made Daisy that promise! Dave and Mother were going to pay for what they had done to Daisy, and Freya was going to make sure of it.

She was going to fight tooth and nail for her sister she would stand at Daisy's side in court and look him and Mother right in her eye while she crumbled. She hoped she would spend the rest of her days in prison and would rot in hell. Freya eventually fell asleep, sobbing at length that night (and many more nights since that phone call), tears of sadness, they were after all close sisters and fighters and they were going to do this together.

Freya woke the next morning, her mind and heart still aching from the night before and from what Daisy had been through, she questioned herself how did she not know but she truly didn't know she just thought Daisy was a quiet kid who just fell into her own world when 'Pops' died. Our poor father, what must of he had to go through.

Freya was even more convinced that Mother had attributed enormously towards his death, the stress she brought to their family ultimately killed you, but she is not going to finish us, we will fight 'Pops' and not be intimidated anymore.

Freya spent the next few days just walking, trying to communicate with the locals and just looking for any type of work however menial, just something to occupy her mind, to be with people and try making new friends. Her new surroundings and lifestyle suited her she sparkled again and glowed with excitement at the prospect of staying here forever.

It would be very hard to leave this place she thought but she could always return she had done it once and would do it again. She had noticed a small handwritten sign in English loosely taped to a tree close by her studio. It was advertising there was a newly renovated vineyard opening next week. There was lots of local talk and interest; many were volunteering to pick the grapes as it was the usual tradition here on this island, they often helped each other in gathering crops etc and expected all to 'chip in' whenever possible in return for some of the cropped produce as payment. Who knows it might one day lead to more permanent work. Freya quickly pencilled her name on the form at the local grocery shop after all what did she have to lose, she would be outside and mixing with the locals getting to know them. Freya was excited and relished the prospect and opportunity, it would be just the boost she needed.

Brett had settled in easily and comfortably into his new surroundings, it had been a long hard struggle but he had enjoyed every moment of it and he was finally getting there.

He had become quite the hero in the village and many admirers as well as friends he had made along the way. He wasn't prepared for romance, not yet anyway, and he was so thankful never to have heard from Cheryl just as exactly as he had anticipated and preferred. He still thought about her, she had been his wife after all and he wished things could have been different.

No doubt she would be settled now and hopefully be happy too. He had also heard from Adam that she had started work as a team leader at a call centre because her divorce settlement could not sustain her lifestyle. How the noble and privileged sometimes have to grasp reality, what Cheryl, the very person who hated the word 'job or work' now having to communicate with the working classes. He had no regrets he genuinely wished her happiness and maybe he still had feelings for her but not in a way that he desired, that had gone a long time ago. And this was now the new Brett but those very thoughts of 'angel' still remained in his inner consciousness. She still visited him in his dreams she kept him strong. If only she was real, she would complete him, but for now he would settle for his dreams and the happy place where he was now, that cloud of uncertainty banished to a distant memory, long gone never to return, at least that's what he hoped.

Brett's new friends helped him get on his feet they were his greatest support they were able to negotiate with the local contractors for better discounts who were more than pleased with the work for a meaningful project that in return would encourage more visitors and, in the process, help the local economy. For him too it was back-breaking hard work, but he relished the task of 'getting stuck in'.

He vowed to repay his friends who helped once the vineyard started making money, but in the meantime, he paid them with a little kindness and bought them food and drink which in the village was relatively cheap. He started to hang out with them treating them to the odd few beers, it was a great start to a new life, he couldn't have wished for anything better. He truly valued and appreciated their friendship they were genuine honest friends with no alternative motives it was a world away from where he had been living. It was a wonderfully simple life and if the vineyard eventually made some money, he was going to support the community after all they had supported him through good and the occasional bad times. Although he spoke little Greek, the language barrier was never a problem and they communicated well; most of the younger generation had been taught English at the village school from an early age and were able to help in translations. Volunteers were coming forward to help mostly women who wanted to get to know him better, Brett didn't mind; he secretly quite liked the attention, he had never experienced that before, word had spread around the village 'single handsome man restoring dilapidated local vineyard' he was becoming quite a celebrity. He was even featured in the local magazine; secretly he was flattered by the attention but was really grateful for everyone's support. He spoke to his mother on a regular basis at the very least twice a week.

She had offered him some extra funding to push on with the works but Brett politely refused as he needed to stand on his own two feet and promised to fly her over once everything was completed.

Life was good for Brett and he was hopeful that anytime soon and probably at the next harvest the vineyard would start to make enough money to cover all his bills and pay the staff a better wage than he currently was giving them. His savings were slowly running out but he was confident the yield at harvest was going to be plentiful and great quality to sell on the bulk to the large consortium. He then would be so much happier, he wanted nothing more life was simple here and it was going to get better he knew it.

The sun rose early that morning and Brett was working in the groves, it was hot but he was acclimatising to the weather now, his body was toned from manual working every day, his skin bronzed and his hair had turned a striking silver blonde bleached with the sun, he was a different man now to the last one he saw in the mirror. He felt truly alive for the first time in his life. Brett was so thirsty and as he turned around to get water that is when he saw her, this could not be happening he closed his eyes tight then opened them again and there right in front of him stood 'ANGEL' long black hair shining in the sun, she was smiling really smiling.

Brett instantly wanted to grab her, kiss her, and tell her everything. This was the woman who had been in his dreams for so many years, the woman he loved, she was real, alive and so very beautiful, the vision as he exactly had pictured in his dreams.

Freya stood staring for what seemed a lifetime, she felt she knew this man, what was happening to her, is this what she had been waiting for all her life too? Freya held out her hand and spoke softly, just as Brett imagined she would.

"Hello, my name is…"

"I already know," Brett replied, "welcome home."

To be continued…